D0659449

RAINBOW magic®

The Party Fairies

To a very special Jasmine - Miss Jasmine Grewal - with lots of love

Special thanks to Narinder Dhami

ORCHARD BOOKS

First published in Great Britain in 2005 by Orchard Books
This edition published in 2018 by The Watts Publishing Group

3

Copyright © 2018 Rainbow Magic Limited.
Copyright © 2018 HIT Entertainment Limited.
Illustrations copyright © Georgie Ripper, 2005

The moral rights of the author and illustrator have been asserted.
All characters and events in this publication, other than those clearly in the public domain, are fictitious and any resemblance to real persons, living or dead, is purely coincidental.

All rights reserved.
No part of this publication may be reproduced, stored in a retrieval system, or transmitted, in any form or by any means, without the prior permission in writing of the publisher, nor be otherwise circulated in any form of binding or cover other than that in which it is published and without a similar condition including this condition being imposed on the subsequent purchaser.

A CIP catalogue record for this book is available from the British Library.

ISBN 978 1 84362 824 8

Printed in Great Britain by Clays Ltd, Elcograf S.p.A

The paper and board used in this book are made from wood from responsible sources

Orchard Books
An imprint of Hachette Children's Group
Part of The Watts Publishing Group Limited
Carmelite House, 50 Victoria Embankment, London EC4Y 0DZ

An Hachette UK Company
www.hachette.co.uk
www.hachettechildrens.co.uk

Jasmine the Present Fairy

by Daisy Meadows

illustrated by Georgie Ripper

Join the **Rainbow Magic Reading Challenge**!

Read the story and collect your fairy points to climb the Reading Rainbow at the back of the book.

This book is worth 5 points.

The Fairyland Palace
Clearing
The Village Hall
Twisty Lane
Wetherbury Village

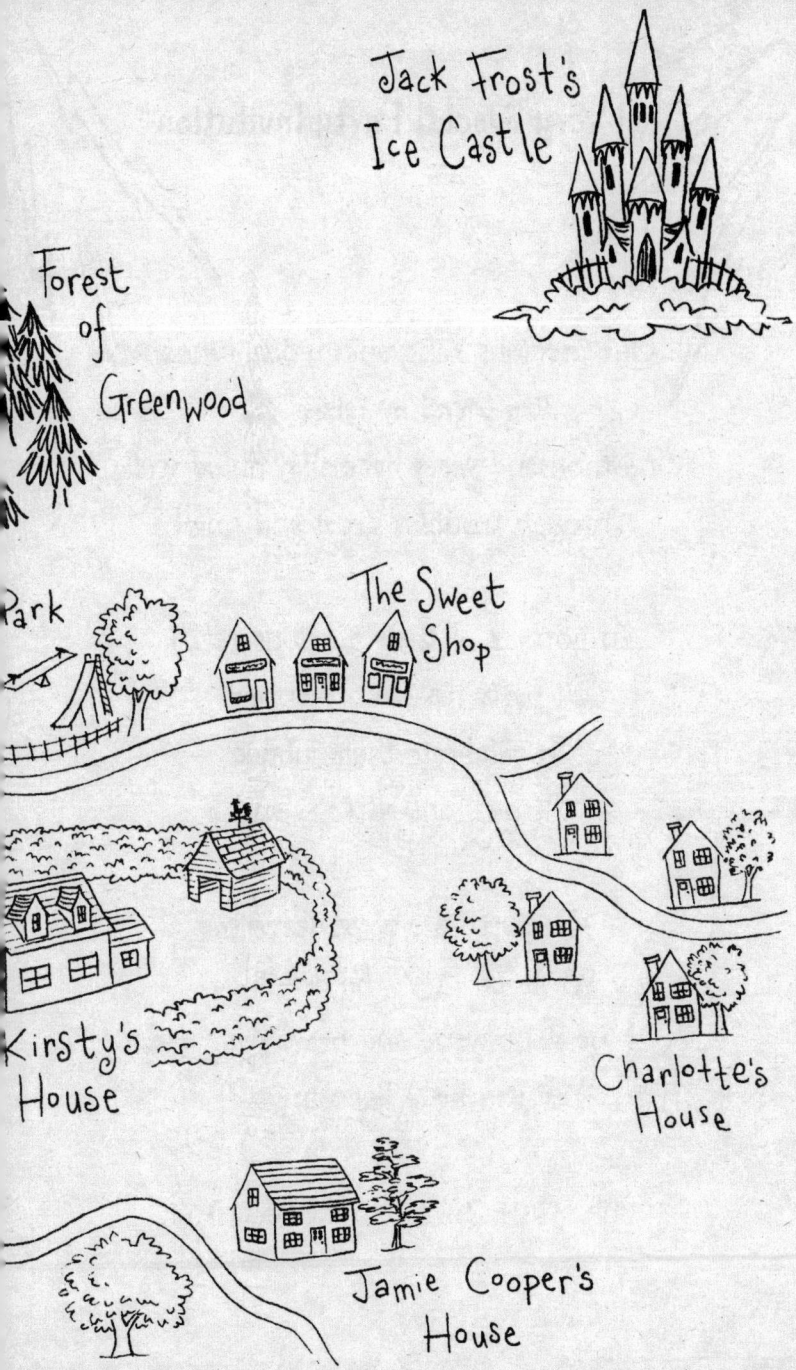
Jack Frost's
Ice Castle
Forest
of
Greenwood
Park
The Sweet
Shop
Kirsty's
House
Charlotte's
House
Jamie Cooper's
House

A Very Special Party Invitation

Our gracious King and gentle Queen
Are loved by fairies all.
One thousand years have they ruled well,
Through troubles great and small.

In honour of their glorious reign
A party has been planned,
To celebrate their jubilee
Throughout all Fairyland.

The party is a royal surprise,
We hope they'll be delighted.
So shine your wand and press your dress...
For you have been invited!

RSVP: HRH THE FAIRY GODMOTHER

Contents

A Special Street Party	9
Unlucky Dip!	23
Girls on the Run	35
All Wrapped Up	47
Fairyland Fun	53
Party Time!	65

A Special Street Party

"Look at all these stalls, Rachel," Kirsty Tate said, pointing down the street where she lived. "This is going to be a great party!"

All of Kirsty's neighbours were bustling around setting up stalls outside their houses. There were all sorts of things going on, from games and raffles to stalls selling bric-a-brac and cakes. Delicious smells wafted towards the girls, from the barbecue at the other end of the street. The road was closed to traffic, and people were already milling around in the sunshine, enjoying the fête.

"I think having a street party is a great idea," Rachel Walker, Kirsty's best friend, said with a grin. "I wish we had one in our street back home." Rachel had come to stay with Kirsty for a week of the Easter holidays.

Kirsty was opening the last box of books. "We'd better hurry and put these on the stall," she said. "Lots of people are arriving now."

"I'm glad the party is today, before I go home tomorrow," Rachel said, helping Kirsty arrange the books on the stall that Mr and Mrs Tate were running. "I hope we raise loads of money for charity."

"We always do," said Kirsty happily, stacking the books neatly. "Lots of people come to the party from all over town. But..." she lowered her voice, "...we'll have to be extra-careful this year, won't we?"

Rachel nodded solemnly. "Yes," she agreed. "A party means we must keep our eyes open for goblin mischief!"

Rachel and Kirsty shared a wonderful secret. They had become friends with the fairies and now, whenever their fairy friends were in trouble, Rachel and Kirsty were happy to help. The cause of the trouble was usually cold, spiky Jack Frost, who had been banished to his ice castle by the King and Queen of Fairyland. This time Jack Frost was determined to ruin the secret party which the Fairy Godmother and the seven Party Fairies were planning for the Fairy King and Queen's 1000th jubilee.

Jack Frost had sent his mean goblin servants into the human world to spoil as many parties as they could.

When the Party Fairies flew to the rescue, the goblins tried to steal their magic party bags so that Jack Frost could use their special magic to throw a fabulous party of his own! But Rachel and Kirsty had managed to stop the goblins so far, and help six of the Party Fairies to keep their party bags safe.

"I'm not going to let Jack Frost's goblins spoil our street party," Kirsty said in a determined voice. "Or the King and Queen's jubilee."

Rachel nodded in agreement as Kirsty's parents hurried towards them.

"You have done well," Mrs Tate smiled, admiring the neat piles of books.

"I think you two girls have worked hard enough," Mr Tate added, as customers began to gather round the stall. "You can go and explore the fête."

"Great!" Kirsty whispered to Rachel, as they walked away. "Now we've got a chance to look for goblins!"

The girls wandered happily through the crowds. There were lots of games, such as darts, hook-a-duck and a tombola, and there were tables piled with bric-a-brac, toys, home-made jams, and other things for sale.

Rachel stopped at a cake stall, her mouth watering as she looked at the delicious display of tarts, sponges and pies. "Cherry the Cake Fairy would be proud of those," she laughed.

"There's no sign of any goblin mischief," said Kirsty. "Shall we have a go on the tombola?"

The tombola was manned by one of Kirsty's neighbours, Mr Cooper, and there was already a queue. Kirsty and Rachel stood behind a little girl holding her mum's hand.

The girl was staring up at the prizes on the shelves behind the tombola machine. "I hope I win a cuddly toy, Mummy," she said excitedly.

"Any ticket ending in four wins a prize!" called Mr Cooper, spinning the tombola round.

Rachel and Kirsty watched as the little girl pulled out a purple ticket. She unfolded it carefully.

"Mummy, I won!" she gasped. "It's number 214."

"Well done!" her mum laughed.

"Let's hope it's a soft toy," Rachel whispered to Kirsty, as the little girl handed Mr Cooper the ticket.

But sharp-eyed Kirsty had already spotted the prize with purple ticket 214 pinned to it. "It's not," she said, pointing. "Look."

The prize was a blue, plastic apron with a picture of a fluffy, white kitten on the front. Kirsty hoped the little girl wouldn't be too disappointed.

"Right, let me find your prize," said Mr Cooper, scanning the shelves. "It's here somewhere..."

But just before he spotted the apron, something magical happened. Rachel and Kirsty saw a shower of blue sparkles appear from thin air and whirl around the apron. The next moment, the apron had vanished and in its place sat a fluffy, white toy kitten, with a blue satin bow around its neck. Pinned to the bow was purple ticket 214.

"I've won the white kitten!" the little girl cried joyfully.

Looking puzzled, Mr Cooper lifted the toy down. "I don't remember seeing that prize before," he murmured.

Kirsty and Rachel grinned at each other as Mr Cooper handed the kitten to the delighted little girl.

"That was fairy magic," whispered Kirsty.

Rachel nodded. "And that means there must be a Party Fairy very nearby!"

The little girl skipped off happily, clutching her prize, while Kirsty and Rachel slipped behind the tombola stall to look for the fairy. They couldn't see any sign of her.

"Rachel! Kirsty!" The girls suddenly heard a silvery voice calling from above their heads. "I'm up here!"

The girls looked up at a string of coloured flags tied to the top of the stall, and there was Jasmine the Present Fairy, balancing on the string like an acrobat on a tightrope!

"Hello," Kirsty and Rachel called, smiling up at her.

Jasmine fluttered down to join them, her straight brown hair flying out behind her. She wore a long, blue skirt with a fluted hemline that swirled around her ankles, and a cropped top in the same shade of blue. On her feet were dark blue ballet shoes with satin ribbons, and in her hand she carried a glittering blue wand.

"I'm here to make sure that your street party goes well," she explained, "and that all the prizes are as perfect as possible." She smiled at Rachel and Kirsty. "And that means making sure no naughty goblins try to ruin the party!" she added in a determined voice.

"Have you seen any goblins?" Rachel asked anxiously.

"No—" Jasmine began, but she was interrupted by the sound of someone crying loudly. It came from the lucky dip, next to the tombola.

"Someone sounds upset," Kirsty whispered. "Maybe we'd better take a look." Jasmine flew down and hid on Rachel's shoulder behind her hair.

Then they hurried over to join the queue at the lucky dip. A little boy was standing by the bran tub, crying bitterly with a toy plane in his hand.

"I loved the plane when I unwrapped it," the boy wailed. "But look, Dad, the wings are broken!"

"This could be goblin trouble," Jasmine whispered in Rachel's ear.

"I'm very sorry," said the man at the lucky dip stall. "I tell you what, why don't you pull out another parcel for free?"

The boy stopped crying immediately. "Thank you," he beamed.

Rachel, Kirsty and Jasmine watched as the little boy put his hand into the bran tub and pulled out a small parcel. He unwrapped it eagerly, but they all stared in horror when a mouldy, old apple fell out!

"Oh, no!" Jasmine gasped.

The little boy began to cry again.

Meanwhile, the stallholder was looking very flustered. "I think somebody's playing a silly joke on me!" he said crossly. "Don't cry." He patted the little boy on the shoulder. "Have another go."

Rachel, Kirsty and Jasmine watched anxiously as the boy pulled out his third parcel. This time he unwrapped a toy car without any wheels!

"All the presents in the lucky dip are spoiled," Kirsty whispered to Rachel and Jasmine. "What are we going to do?"

The little boy was about to burst into tears again, but the kind stallholder saved the day.

"Look," he said, leaning across to the hook-a-duck stall next door, which he was also running. "I'll give you one of these prizes instead." And he handed the boy a shiny bat and ball set.

"Great!" the boy said happily, showing it to his dad as they walked away.

"This is definitely goblin mischief!" Jasmine said as the man bent over the bran tub and began looking through it. "But I'll soon set things right with my party magic."

"That's exactly what the goblin will be hoping for," Kirsty hissed, looking worried. "Don't get your party bag out – he'll be waiting for a chance to steal it!"

"I can't help that," Jasmine whispered, glancing at the boys and girls behind them. "The children will be so disappointed if I don't fix the lucky dip."

"Well, we'll help," Rachel said. "Kirsty, let's make sure the stall owner doesn't notice Jasmine at work. And keep your eyes peeled for goblins."

The man was looking very glum. "I don't think you should have a go, girls," he said. "I may have to close the lucky dip."

"No, don't do that," Rachel said quickly. "I'd like a go on your hook-a-duck stall. What do I have to do?"

While the man was talking to Rachel, Jasmine slid quietly off her shoulder and flew down to the edge of the bran tub. Meanwhile, Kirsty stood right in front of the tub so that nobody in the queue could see what was happening. She was looking out for goblins too.

Quickly, Jasmine opened her party bag and took out a handful of sparkling blue fairy dust, shaped like tiny bows. She sprinkled it over the bran tub and gave a sigh of relief. "All done!" she whispered to Kirsty.

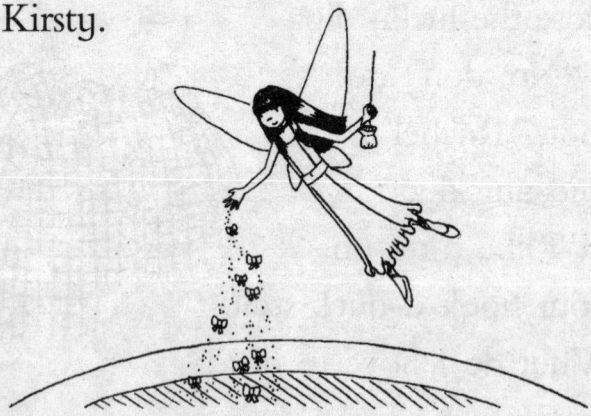

But just then there was a scrabbling noise from *inside* the bran tub. Suddenly, a big green goblin popped up and snatched at Jasmine's party bag.

"Oh!" Jasmine and Kirsty gasped together as the goblin lunged towards them.

Luckily, Jasmine was too quick for him and she whisked the party bag out of his reach. Muttering crossly, the goblin leapt out of the bran tub and darted out of sight behind the stall.

Still shaking with fright, Jasmine fluttered up to sit on Kirsty's shoulder but as she landed, her party bag slipped from her trembling fingers. It fell straight into the lucky dip and disappeared amidst the sawdust.

"Oh, no!" Kirsty groaned.

Over the shoulder of the stallholder, Rachel had seen what was happening. Somehow they had to get Jasmine's party bag back – and fast. "Er, actually I don't want a go on the hook-a-duck," she said quickly. "I think I'll have a go on the lucky dip, after all."

The man looked amazed. "Are you sure?" he asked. "It doesn't seem very lucky at the moment."

"Quite sure," Rachel said firmly.

"Me too," Kirsty added, guessing what Rachel was up to.

The two girls handed over their money. Kirsty went first and Rachel, Jasmine and the stallholder watched as she felt around inside the tub. Her fingers closed over something and she pulled it out. But it was one of the wrapped presents, not Jasmine's party bag. Inside the parcel was a beautiful blue mini-kite.

"At least the presents are OK now," Jasmine whispered in Kirsty's ear.

"Your turn," said the stallholder, looking at Rachel. But just then one of the children at the hook-a-duck stall gave a cry of alarm. He had accidentally got his fishing-rod caught in a string of flags! The stallholder went to help, and Rachel leaned over the bran tub. But just as Rachel was making her lucky dip, Kirsty gave a gasp of horror.

"Watch out!" she whispered. "The goblin is climbing up the table leg!"

Sure enough, the goblin was clambering up the leg of the table back towards the bran tub, with a very determined look on his face.

"There's only your dip left, Rachel," Kirsty whispered anxiously. "You must get Jasmine's party bag before the goblin does!"

Quickly, Rachel plunged her hand into the sawdust and began to feel around. She wondered how she would know when she'd found the party bag, but then she felt something tingle under her fingers. "Fairy magic!" Rachel said to herself, and she drew the object out.

Both girls gasped with relief – it was Jasmine's party bag.

"Hurrah!" Jasmine cried happily.

"Thanks, Rachel."

Just then the goblin peered over the edge of the bran tub. He grinned when he saw the party bag and made another grab for it, but Rachel managed to jump away from him, clutching the bag tightly.

"Let's get out of here," Kirsty suggested. "Quick, back to my house!"

The girls and Jasmine darted behind the stall and ran away from the fête towards the Tates' house. But the goblin chased after them.

Rachel glanced over her shoulder. "He's not far behind!" she panted.

They reached the house and Kirsty let them in through the front door. But the goblin was charging towards them and the girls only just managed to slam the door shut in time. "We have to get rid of that goblin," Jasmine said urgently.

"I've got an idea!" Kirsty declared suddenly. "Rachel, you guard the door. Jasmine, follow me."

Rachel nodded and waited by the front door as Jasmine and Kirsty dashed into the living-room.

Then a tiny sound made Rachel jump.

Her heart thumping, Rachel looked round. She smiled to see Pearl, Kirsty's black and white kitten, sitting at the top of the stairs, watching her.

But then Rachel heard something else. It was the noise of the catflap in the kitchen door creaking open. Rachel frowned. If Pearl was sitting on the stairs, then who was coming in?

She crept along the hall towards the kitchen and spotted...the goblin, climbing in through the catflap.

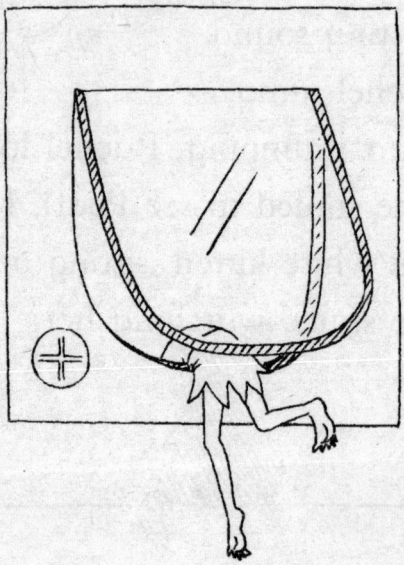

"Kirsty! Jasmine!" she shouted. "Look out, the goblin's coming!"

In the living-room, Jasmine looked at Kirsty in alarm. "What shall we do?" she cried.

But Kirsty was picking up an empty cardboard box which had been full of books for the stall. "If we can make the goblin believe your party bag is in this box, we might be able to trap him inside!" she said.

"Can you lay a trail of magic sparkles leading into the box?"

"I can do better than that!" Jasmine replied eagerly. She opened her party bag and sprinkled some glittering fairy dust onto the cardboard. Immediately, it changed into a beautiful blue gift box, with a lovely golden ribbon lying beside it. Then Jasmine laid the trail of fairy dust into the box and she and Kirsty dived out of sight behind the sofa.

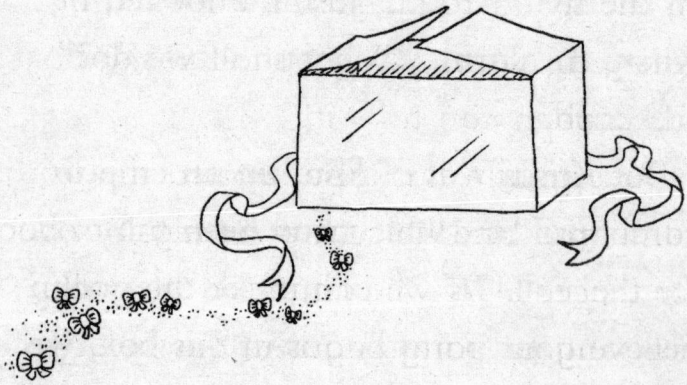

No sooner were Kirsty and Jasmine in hiding than the goblin dashed into the living-room and skidded to a halt, closely followed by Rachel.

Poor Rachel couldn't believe her eyes when she saw the trail of fairy dust and no sign of Kirsty and Jasmine. "Oh, no!" she gasped. "If the party bag is in the box, the goblin can take it!"

The goblin had also spotted the fairy dust trail and he was beaming all over his face. "Ha!" he chuckled gleefully, sticking his tongue out at Rachel. "Jack Frost is going to be very pleased with me when I take him a magic party bag!" And, still chuckling, he crawled into the box.

Immediately, Jasmine and Kirsty rushed out from behind the sofa. Rachel, who wasn't expecting it, almost jumped out of her skin. "Quick, Rachel!" cried Kirsty, "Help me close the box!"

Rachel sprang forward, and she and Kirsty shut the lid.

Then Jasmine waved her wand, and the gold ribbon floated up into the air and tied itself firmly around the box.

There was a cry of rage from inside as the goblin realised he'd been tricked.

"So that's what you were up to!" Rachel laughed.

"Let me out!" the goblin roared.

"I don't think so," Kirsty replied.

"Shall we send the goblin back to Jack Frost by fairy magic mail?" Jasmine suggested.

The girls nodded and Jasmine waved her wand again. There was a shower of fairy dust and a label appeared on the box. It said "Jack Frost, Ice Castle" in big letters. Then, in another swirl of glittering magic, the parcel vanished completely.

Kirsty turned to Rachel. "We did it!" she beamed. "We saved all the Party Fairies' magic party bags!"

"That means the jubilee party for our King and Queen can go ahead without any more trouble from Jack Frost," Jasmine declared happily. "And it's all thanks to you two."

Kirsty and Rachel grinned proudly at each other.

Then Kirsty stared. "Look!" she cried, pointing at the window.

A rainbow of shimmering colours was streaming through the glass. The girls blinked in wonder as one end of the beautiful rainbow came to rest on the floor beside them.

"It's the magic rainbow to take us to Fairyland!" Rachel breathed.

"Remember, Kirsty? Bertram said the Fairy Godmother would send a rainbow for us when it was time for the jubilee party."

"Oh!" Kirsty gasped. "But we're not ready! We haven't got our party clothes on."

Jasmine laughed. "Just step onto the end of the rainbow, girls," she told them. "We Party Fairies will soon sort you out when you get to Fairyland." She waved her wand. "See you very soon!" she called, as she vanished in a swirl of glitter.

"Come on, Kirsty," Rachel said, taking her friend's hand.

Together, the girls stepped carefully into the rainbow. Immediately, there was a whooshing sound, and they were surrounded by glittering golden fairy dust as the rainbow whisked them away.

"Here they are!" called a joyful voice.

As the golden sparkles cleared, the girls found themselves in the Great Hall of the Party Workshop in Fairyland. They were already fairy-sized themselves, with glittering wings on their backs. And there was Jasmine and the other six Party Fairies smiling at them.

"Welcome to the party!" they cried.

"Wow!" Rachel exclaimed, looking round.

Last time the girls had been there, the Party Fairies had been busy with preparations, but now everything was ready. All the fairies were there to welcome the King and Queen, dressed in their best party outfits. Grace the Glitter Fairy had been busy decorating the hall with sparkling streamers, rainbow balloons and jewelled lanterns. There were also

tiny, white fairy lights strung all over the ceiling. Rachel and Kirsty had never seen anything so beautiful. In one corner, the frog orchestra was playing a cheerful tune. In another, presents were piled up, all beautifully wrapped by Jasmine and tied with satin bows in rainbow colours. There were bowls of sweets placed here and there, and on a golden table stood a huge cake shaped like the King and Queen's palace.

Rachel and Kirsty were amused to see the goblin who had tried to steal Cherry the Cake Fairy's party bag, fussing over the cake.

"Now don't touch the icing," he was telling the fairies standing round the table. "I spent ages making sure it looked exactly like the palace!"

"He seems to be enjoying himself," Rachel whispered to Kirsty.

"I'm so happy to see you, girls," the Fairy Godmother declared as she hurried towards them. Her green eyes shone with happiness and the jewels on her golden dress twinkled in the candlelight. "We're so grateful to you for making sure our party wasn't ruined by Jack Frost!" She turned to Phoebe the Fashion Fairy. "I think Phoebe has something for you."

"I do!" Phoebe laughed. "How about some beautiful new dresses for the party, girls?"

"Oh, yes please!" Kirsty and Rachel cried together.

Phoebe smiled and threw a handful of sparkling fairy dust over them. Both girls closed their eyes.

Kirsty was the first to open them again. "Oh, Rachel!" she gasped. "These are the most beautiful dresses I've ever seen!"

Rachel opened her eyes to see Kirsty wearing a long, sparkling rose-pink and gold dress, with pink ballet shoes and a glittering pink tiara. Rachel wore the same, but her outfit was in shimmering lilac and silver. "Thank you, Phoebe—" the girls began.

But before they could say any more, a little fairy zoomed into the Great Hall, panting with excitement. "The King and Queen are here!" she cried.

Everyone began to talk at once, but the Fairy Godmother raised her wand for silence. "Now remember," she called, "when the King and Queen get out of their carriage, everybody shouts, 'SURPRISE!'"

Rachel, Kirsty and all the fairies crowded around the door.

A shining crystal carriage, pulled by six white unicorns and driven by Bertram, the frog footman, was making its way towards them. The carriage stopped and Bertram hopped down to open the door. Out stepped the Fairy King and Queen.

"SURPRISE!" shouted everybody – Rachel and Kirsty loudest of all.

The King and Queen looked puzzled

for a moment, but then they saw the golden banner which hung over the castle door: Congratulations to our beloved King Oberon and Queen Titania on their 1000th jubilee!

"Oh!" the Queen gasped, looking delighted. "How wonderful!"

"I think our Party Fairies have had a hand in this," the King beamed joyfully.

The Fairy Godmother stepped forward. "Welcome, King Oberon and Queen Titania!" she announced. "But the Party Fairies aren't the only ones who have helped to make this party special. We must also thank our friends, Rachel and Kirsty." And she turned to smile at the girls. "Once again they have saved us from Jack Frost's mischief.

"Thank you, girls," said the King warmly. "You must tell us the whole story later."

"You both look beautiful," the Queen added with a smile. "Now, let's forget all about Jack Frost, and enjoy the party!"

Rachel and Kirsty had never been to such a party in their lives. The frog orchestra played catchy tunes, specially created by Melodie the Music Fairy, and all the fairies danced and fluttered around like colourful butterflies.

Then there were party games, organised by Polly the Party Fun Fairy: Pass the Magic Parcel, Musical Magical Chairs and many more.

The sweets made by Honey the Sweet Fairy were so delicious that Rachel and Kirsty just couldn't stop eating the Strawberry Sparkles.

After the games, everyone gathered round to watch the King and Queen open their presents and then cut the wonderful cake, made by Cherry and iced by the goblin. All too soon, the party was over.

"I hope you've had a good time, girls," Queen Titania said, smiling at Rachel and Kirsty.

"It was great!" Rachel declared.

"The best party ever!" Kirsty added.

"It's time for you to go home now," the Queen went on. She waved her wand and a shimmering rainbow appeared beside them. "But before you go, I think the Party Fairies have something for you."

Jasmine and Cherry flew forward.

"These are from all of us!" Jasmine said, handing Kirsty a pink, sparkly party bag, while Cherry gave Rachel a lilac one.

"Don't look in them till you get home."

"Thank you," Kirsty and Rachel replied, waving at their friends. "See you again soon, we hope."

"Goodbye!" answered all the fairies.

And with the voices of their fairy friends ringing in their ears, the girls stepped into the rainbow. Moments later, they found themselves in the Tates' kitchen, restored to their usual size and wearing their normal clothes once more.

"Oh, that was magical!" Kirsty sighed happily.

Rachel was already opening her party bag. "Look, Kirsty!" she exclaimed in delight.

The bags were full of presents from their Party Fairy friends. There was a piece of jubilee cake from Cherry, a fairy music CD from Melodie, a tub of glittery lip gloss from Grace, a silk bag of sweets from Honey, a pack of magic playing cards from Polly and a sparkly bracelet from Phoebe. And Jasmine had given them each a golden jewellery box with a revolving fairy on top to put all their presents in.

Rachel and Kirsty couldn't believe their eyes.

"We must be the luckiest girls in the world," Rachel sighed.

"And we can still enjoy the rest of the street party, too," Kirsty added.

Later that night, the girls lay in their beds in Kirsty's room, still too excited to sleep. The jewellery boxes, filled with presents, sat on the dressing-table.

"It's sad that I have to go home tomorrow," Rachel said with a yawn. "But I've really enjoyed our latest fairy adventure and we'll see each other again soon?"

"Me too," Kirsty agreed, starting to feel sleepy at last. She closed her eyes.

There was silence for a few moments. Then, "I can hear something," Rachel said. "It's coming from our jewellery boxes!"

The soft, tinkling sound of party music filled the room.

"Fairy magic!" Kirsty said happily, snuggling down under her duvet. "Goodnight, Rachel."

Meet the Friendship Fairies

When Jack Frost steals the Friendship Fairies' magical objects, BFFs everywhere are in trouble! Can Rachel and Kirsty help save the magic of friendship?

www.rainbowmagicbooks.co.uk

Calling all parents, carers and teachers!
The Rainbow Magic fairies are here to help your child enter the magical world of reading. Whatever reading stage they are at, there's a Rainbow Magic book for everyone! Here is Lydia the Reading Fairy's guide to supporting your child's journey at all levels.

1

Starting Out

Our Rainbow Magic Beginner Readers are perfect for first-time readers who are just beginning to develop reading skills and confidence. Approved by teachers, they contain a full range of educational levelling, as well as lively full-colour illustrations.

2

Developing Readers

Rainbow Magic Early Readers contain longer stories and wider vocabulary for building stamina and growing confidence. These are adaptations of our most popular Rainbow Magic stories, specially developed for younger readers in conjunction with an Early Years reading consultant, with full-colour illustrations.

3

Going Solo

The Rainbow Magic chapter books – a mixture of series and one-off specials – contain accessible writing to encourage your child to venture into reading independently. These highly collectible and much-loved magical stories inspire a love of reading to last a lifetime.

www.rainbowmagicbooks.co.uk

"Rainbow Magic got my daughter reading chapter books. Great sparkly covers, cute fairies and traditional stories full of magic that she found impossible to put down" – Mother of Edie (6 years)

"Florence LOVES the Rainbow Magic books. She really enjoys reading now" – Mother of Florence (6 years)

The Rainbow Magic Reading Challenge

Well done, fairy friend – you have completed the book!
This book was worth 5 points.

See how far you have climbed on the
Reading Rainbow opposite.

The more books you read, the more points you will get, and the closer you will be to becoming a Fairy Princess!

How to get your Reading Rainbow

1. Cut out the coin below
2. Go to the Rainbow Magic website
3. Download and print out your poster
4. Add your coin and climb up the Reading Rainbow!

There's all this and lots more at
www.rainbowmagicbooks.co.uk

You'll find activities, competitions, stories, a special newsletter and complete profiles of all the Rainbow Magic fairies. Find a fairy with your name!